# DATE DUE

| | | | |
|---|---|---|---|
| | | | |
| | | | |
| | | | |
| | | | |
| | | | |
| | | | |
| | | | |
| | | | |
| | | | |
| | | | |
| | | | |
| | | | |
| | | | |
| | | | |
| | | | |
| | | | |
| | | | |

# BARTLETT BROTHERS
## THE FRANKENSTEIN PROJECT
### ROGER ELWOOD

WORD PUBLISHING
Dallas·London·Vancouver·Melbourne

THE FRANKENSTEIN PROJECT

Copyright © 1991 by Roger Elwood.

Edited by Beverly Phillips

**Library of Congress Cataloging-in-Publication Data**

Elwood, Roger.
     The Frankenstein Project / Roger Elwood.
        p.  cm.—(The Bartlett brothers)
     Summary: A visit to a hospitalized friend plunges the Bartlett brothers into a mysterious scientific world that none of them may leave alive.
     ISBN 0–8499–3303–X
     [1. Brothers—Fiction.  2. Mystery and detective stories.]
I. Title.  II. Series: Elwood, Roger. Bartlett brothers.
PZ7. E554Fr  1991
[Fic]—dc20                                91–21960
                                               CIP
                                               AC

*Printed in the United States of America*

3 4 5 6 7 8 9 LBM 7 6 5 4 3

TO GIGI
1980–1991
Now on her own
angelwalk

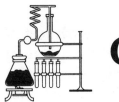 # One

"**D**id you see that?" Ryan Bartlett asked.

"What do you mean?" his brother Chad replied. "It's dark around here . . . hard to see much of anything."

He was right about that. The grounds of Woodview Rehabilitation Hospital, where they had been visiting, were not well lit. It was as though everything and everyone went into some kind of cocoon after a certain hour, and there was no need to waste electricity on lighting with nobody up and about to use it.

"There! Look!" Ryan exclaimed. "Stop the car. . . ."

Still a good way from the main gate, Chad hit the brakes. His brother opened the door and jumped out.

*I saw it, I really did,* Ryan told himself, dashing toward the woods. *I know I didn't imagine it.*

Running.

There! Ahead!

The hospital was in a rural area northwest of Los Angeles and somewhat inland from Malibu Beach. Set in the midst of what might be called a small forest, it was almost totally isolated from the noise and pollution found in the cities.

The Bartlett brothers had gone there to see a friend, but had to leave—it was past eight o'clock, and visiting hours were over.

*So white,* Ryan thought.

Oh, yes.

A very white face peered at him through the darkness, eyes red-rimmed.

He spotted some movement again, a blur directly ahead of where he was standing.

Into the trees!

Ryan continued to follow the mysterious figure. He knew he was acting very foolish. And yet, before now, he had prided himself on being the sensible brother. His mind was like the computer system at which he spent so much time.

That was true, but he never expected to see that face, that sad, round child's face.

A little girl. . . .

She turned, only for a second, before she disappeared into the thick maze of trees.

Crying.

She was crying, moonlight reflecting off tears that trickled down her pale, pale cheeks.

Ryan followed her. Now he could hear movement in back of him as well. Chad was probably following him.

As Ryan entered the small section of trees, mental images from his own earlier years came instantly back to him. They were from a dream he used to have. It was one that involved being lost in a place like that one, with every tree branch casting a threatening-looking shadow across his path as he looked nervously from side to side.

*How much I've really grown up since then,* he kidded himself. *Yeah, sure!*

He stopped in his tracks.

Only the sounds behind him could be heard now.

Otherwise—.

His heart suddenly beat several times faster than normal as he saw that face again!

But not just *that* face!

Others.

Some larger. A couple even smaller.

At least six faces were peering out from the thick vegetation at him.

All of them were chalky white like the first. And all seemed so sad.

Then gone.

All vanished, followed by the rustling of autumn leaves. Some dead branches on the ground being crushed underfoot.

Suddenly a hand came down firmly on his shoulder!

Ryan jumped and let out a low yell as he spun around.

"Chad!"

"Hey, what's going on, Ryan?" he asked.

"Did you see them?"

Chad looked as though he didn't want to answer his brother's question.

"You did, didn't you?" Ryan persisted.

Chad nodded.

"I guess I hesitated because I remember that strange message you intercepted a few months ago on your computer, Ryan. It turned out that terrorists were involved. We ended up trapped on a wild helicopter ride near a nuclear power plant, with Dad hanging out one door. And approaching Air Force fighter planes were about ready to blow us out of the sky!"

"So, you think I'm being true to form because I want to see what *this* is all about, is that it?"

Chad gulped a couple of times.

"Yes, and so do I. Though that may surprise you, little brother," he admitted, smiling. "But . . . but—"

"But what?" Ryan asked.

"We should *tell* somebody. Who knows what may be going on?"

"And you think they're going to believe us?"

"Dad will."

"He's off on another assignment."

Chad's shoulders slumped.

"But we don't know where they went," he said.

"I'm sure there are plenty of tracks," Ryan said. "I heard twigs breaking. If it were daytime, we'd have no trouble following them."

Chad had to agree with his brother.

"Yes, but it's not, and we have to get back home."

"Wonder where they went?" Ryan said. "I counted at least half a dozen faces."

Chad rubbed his arm. A sudden chill had touched it and was starting to spread to the rest of his body.

*They looked like little ghosts,* he thought. *But then there is no such thing. . . .*

In the moonlight he was certain he could make out some tracks.

Real.

We didn't both imagine them, that's for sure, he told himself.

Chad bent down and picked up something he saw shining in the pale light.

A heart-shaped locket.

"What's that?" Ryan asked.

Chad showed it to him.

"Look inside," Ryan said. "Maybe there's some kind of identification."

Inside were engraved just a few words:

*To Laurene:*
*Even in the darkness, your light shines.*
*Mom and Dad*

"Doesn't sound so strange, does it?" Chad commented, a little embarrassed that he had acted almost as alarmed as his little brother had. He sure hoped that Ryan wouldn't somehow throw this up to him later.

*Great example I am!* he thought.

"You're right," Ryan said. "It's none of our business, really."

"I'll keep the locket until we come back again in a couple of weeks. Maybe Barney or someone at the hospital will know the owner."

As they walked back to the car, Ryan was thinking of their friend Barney, who was undergoing the final stages of intense physical therapy at that private hospital.

Barney Fitzsimmons, a retired police officer . . .

*He's there because of us,* Ryan told himself. *He was injured trying to protect us from the terrorists. We've been so worried about him. Praise God that he is going to make it!*

Ryan would never forget the events of that night months earlier. After being cornered by some terrorists, his brother and he had tried to hide in the attic of Barney's house. They could hear him trying to fight off the men who were after the two of them. There were shots. They thought Barney had been killed. He wasn't, but he had been hurt, badly. It had taken months of therapy in order for Barney to be able to walk normally again.

*We try to visit Barney whenever we can. I really wish, though, it were more often. . . .*

Ryan knew there wasn't any honest reason for feeling guilty about any of that.

And yet—

"Chad?" he asked.

"Yeah," his brother replied as they were getting into their car. "What is it, Ryan?"

"Let's make it sooner than two weeks this time."

"Because of what we saw? Or Barney?"

"Barney."

"Are you so sure, Ryan?"

Ryan hesitated, images of those strange little children sharp in his mind.

"Both," he replied honestly. "Because of Barney *and,* yeah, what we saw just now."

"Fine with me."

As they drove away, Ryan turned just for a moment and looked back, still not able to clear what he had seen from his mind.

"Ryan, are you all right?" Chad asked.

"I'll be okay," Ryan said, but not with any energy.

"Look, forget about that minding-our-business stuff. We *should* find out something," Chad reassured himself and Ryan at the same time. "Maybe some of those . . . those kids, whatever they are, whatever's wrong with them, need our help. We'll start asking questions in the morning. But please, do your big brother a favor: Don't let what we saw bother you."

"Yeah. . . ."

Ryan smiled, realizing that Chad was doing his best to make him feel a little better.

He closed his eyes but knew that he wouldn't be able to take a nap on the way back home. He was nowhere near relaxed enough. And all he could see were those very white faces peering through the darkness, eyes red-rimmed. . . .

Ryan shivered, realizing he was overreacting but unable to restrain himself very much.

*Who are you?* he thought, not certain that he wanted to find out the answer.

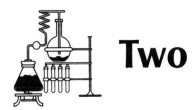

# Two

**R**yan had a full medical encyclopedia and other reference books stored on a CD-ROM disk that he slipped carefully into a special slot in the front of his computer. Minutes before, as soon as their car had pulled in the driveway, he had raced to his bedroom.

*What could make someone look like that?* he wondered, recalling the haunting white faces.

*I've got to find out.*

He knew what he had seen couldn't be the result of anything supernatural. Those figures were not ghosts, trying to make contact with the living.

*They were real, flesh-and-blood boys and girls who left behind crushed leaves and broken twigs . . . and a locket.*

But Ryan also realized that they were not ordinary kids. He had never seen anyone before who looked so white. *Could they be albinos, people who have no pigment in their skin?*

As he started to type some keywords into the computer, which would access the CD-ROM, he hesitated a moment, recalling the expression on those faces.

*Sadness. . . .*

*Each face had looked so sad.*

He had known his own sorrow before, when his mother died. She had been killed suddenly in an explosion just outside their home. A terrorist's bomb blew up when she turned on the ignition of the family car.

Her murderers either had hoped instead to kill Andrew Bartlett, their father, or they had actually intended her cruel death to be a warning.

*Our father, the spy. . . .*

Mr. Bartlett was a secret agent for the CIA, working under cover as a special envoy of the U.S. State Department. He regularly traveled tens of thousands of miles to the Middle East and Africa and the Orient, and other faraway places. Of course, this meant he was home only two or three months a year.

*And you're constantly in danger, Dad. A message could come any time that you had been—.*

He shook his head at that thought, trying to clear his mind and concentrate on the computer screen in front of him.

The trouble was that he didn't altogether know what to look for: Was it a skin condition? A blood disorder?

He scrolled through several categories, not satisfied with the contents of any of them. He was ready to give up when one heading caught his attention:

### GENETICS

*Yes!* he declared to himself.

Within five minutes, he had come across an especially interesting passage on screen:

### Xeroderma pigmentosum
(zēr´-ə-dûr´-mə pig´-mən-tō´-səm)

*What a mouthful!* Ryan thought.

He continued to read about the condition, which was called XP for short and was extremely rare:

*Only one individual in 200,000 is afflicted with it. That means that no more than a thousand Americans have XP. There is no known cure.*

Ryan began to feel ashamed that he had reacted as he did when he saw the children. If, in fact, XP was what they had, it was something they had been born with, because it was an inherited condition. One of their parents would have passed the defective gene on to them.

He read on further:

*XP is often fatal, making its victims acutely vulnerable to skin and eye cancers if they are even briefly exposed to sun or any other source of ultraviolet rays.*

*Maybe that's it,* Ryan said to himself. *Maybe that is why those children were out at night! Their skin is too sensitive to sunlight.*

Ryan shut off his computer and went to bed. But he stayed awake for more than an hour, thinking about pale-faced children with red-rimmed eyes.

# Three

**B**ack home after school, Ryan decided to call Barney Fitzsimmons at the hospital.

"Good to hear your voice!" Barney said enthusiastically. "I really enjoyed our visit yesterday."

"So did we," Ryan assured him. "Barney, you won't believe what happened afterwards."

"Tell me about it."

Ryan told him every detail of the encounter.

Barney didn't say anything for a few seconds after his young friend had finished the story.

"Anything wrong?" Ryan asked.

"Sorry . . ." Barney replied, embarrassed. "I saw one of them a couple of weeks ago."

"You did?"

"Yeah, Ryan. Like you, I thought that one looked very ghostly. I knew the child couldn't be a ghost, of course, but I'd never seen anything like it."

Ryan went on to talk about the possible conditions that forced them to go out only at night.

"XP? I'll ask the doctors here some questions about it. They'll probably be able to tell me something."

"Great, Barney."

"If I find out anything, I'll ring you back. I wonder, though, what's going to come of this, Ryan? I mean, you've been involved in some pretty hair-raising business over the past few years. This new situation must seem pretty dull to you by any comparison."

"I don't know yet. It's just a feeling I have. I don't know what's at the bottom of it."

"No problem, Ryan. I'm kind of interested, too. Seeing kids like that, and now knowing what might be wrong with them . . . well, what I'm trying to say is that maybe we could find out where they came from and spend some time with them, like you guys have been doing with me."

"Sounds like a good idea, Barney. We'll keep in touch."

Ryan hung up the receiver. He knew Barney well enough to sense that there was something the old guy was not telling him.

# Four

**B**arney Fitzsimmons *was shaking when he sat back in the wheelchair, realizing that he hadn't been dreaming. He had truly seen that strange-looking youngster.*

*What he hadn't told Ryan was the rest of the story . . . which had happened two weeks earlier.*

Barney had been sitting in his wheelchair on the patio at the back of the hospital one night, enjoying the almost total quiet. A few crickets could be heard. An owl hooted a couple of times, but that was it.

He felt so peaceful.

Then suddenly there was a very light touch on his left shoulder. And he jumped.

Barney swung the wheelchair around.

One of those pale children.

"What in the—?" he started to say.

The frail-looking little girl just stood there, looking at him.

"Who are you?" Barney asked, finally managing to say something after his nerves calmed down.

She didn't speak.

"You look so sad," he said. "Are you lost?"

She shook her head.

"Where did you come from?" he asked.

She pointed to her left, toward the woods.

"Did you run away from home?"

She frowned, either trying to understand his question or having difficulty in giving him an answer.

"The darkness . . ." she said finally.

He understood the word but not what she meant by it.

Abruptly there was the sound of car doors slamming shut.

Two men were running across the lawn. The little girl cringed as they approached.

Barney wheeled his chair between her and the approaching adults. He knew that he couldn't offer much protection but decided that he had to try, if indeed it was protection that she needed.

The two men stood directly in front of him. They were tall, broad-shouldered and tough-looking.

One of them spoke with a thick Italian accent.

"You've got to come back with us right away, Laurene," he said. "Your father is visiting now. He was very upset when he found that you had run away again."

"Why couldn't he come for her himself?" Barney asked with suspicion.

"Mister, Paul Giovanni owes no one any explanation, *no one!*" the other man snapped.

*Paul Giovanni!*

*Barney knew that name immediately—the head of the leading West Coast Mafia family.*

Practically speaking, Barney understood that he really had no choice. He couldn't keep the men from taking the little girl. As tough-looking as the men were, when the first one had spoken to little Laurene, Barney had not detected any threat or anything of the sort. In fact, the man seemed genuinely concerned for the child's welfare.

"I don't want to go back," Laurene said. "I—."

"You want to hide somewhere until daylight, don't you?" the first man told her. "You want to feel the sun's rays on your beautiful skin."

She nodded, tears streaking down her cheeks.

"But that would kill you, dear child," the man added. "You know what happened to your mother."

She bowed her head as she whispered, "Yes . . . I know."

"Please, come now," the man asked her, his voice more tender than Barney could ever have imagined would be the case.

Laurene walked past the wheelchair and allowed the other man to take her hand. She turned, for a moment, glancing back at Barney. Then the three of them were gone.

*Today after Ryan's call, Barney knew that he had to tell someone. For two weeks now, he had not been able to get the image of little Laurene out of his mind.*

*They were only teenagers, but Ryan and Chad could be trusted. And, because of their father, they were blessed with contacts that even an ex-cop did not have.*

*In the morning he would call and tell the boys the whole thing. . . . There must be a clinic close by which treats the rare XP disease.*

 # Five

**A**re you serious?" Ryan said after listening to Barney Fitzsimmons. "A Mafia don? The leader of some organized crime group on the West Coast who—?"

He stopped himself. His friend's suspicions were pretty wild. How much of what he said could be taken seriously? But the idea of an *XP* clinic nearby did make sense.

"Maybe Chad and I should pay you a visit earlier than we had planned," Ryan suggested.

Barney cautioned him about making too much of the whole thing.

"Besides, what will it prove?" the retired police officer asked. "There's nothing illegal about treating children who happened to be afflicted with XP. And there's always the risk of danger when you go snooping around people who have Mafia connections."

Ryan had to admit that Barney was correct.

There was just no sense getting into trouble on purpose. Over the past year, Chad and he had had enough problems walk right up to them. They certainly didn't need to go looking for any.

It was morning when Ryan got Barney's phone call. Chad had gone to school early to get in more training for an upcoming wrestling competition. So Ryan was alone, except for Miss Stephenson, their English-born housekeeper. Chad would have to grab a quick breakfast on the way to school. But Ryan had time for a fine English breakfast, with poached eggs on English muffins, and orange marmalade smeared across fresh homemade bread.

"You are an amazing cook!" Ryan said with genuine appreciation for all the wonderful meals she had served them through the years.

"Thank you. English food is often underrated," she replied. "But there's nothing any better than Dover sole cooked in Welsh rarebit, stuffed with grapes along with—?"

She hesitated, waiting for him to finish the sentence.

"Yorkshire pudding as a side dish and trifle for dessert," he said, thinking of one of his favorite meals. "Just the thought of it makes me want to go to London again. The three of us could go to-morrow. What do you say about that?"

"Great idea," she told him, "but terrible timing."

Ryan was laughing.

"Your eyes really lit up, though," he said.

"Spring vacation," she suggested. "How about then?"

"We'll do it. Chad and I *love* London."

Miss Stephenson was about to leave the breakfast nook when Ryan said, "Saw some strange kids a couple of nights ago. I'd really like to tell you about what happened."

"Of course," she said, returning to the table and sitting down in a chair opposite Ryan.

When Ryan had finished telling her about the incident, he added the information that Barney had provided.

"We had Mafia types in London," she said. "They're not just Italian anymore, you know. There are *Mafioso* from a variety of nationalities. Of course, some of the old ones still involved dislike what they consider to be the racial pollution of their secret society. But all Mafia groups, no matter what their nationality, rule by force, by bribes, by corruption at various levels of government. They are a dirty, awful bunch, but—."

She leaned forward on her elbows.

"—there is one thing that is very, very true about members of the Mafia. They are *devoted* to their families. For example, if someone insults the mother of a Mafia godfather (that's another name for the powerful family leader), you can be sure he'll pay for it. Whoever it is will be either killed or beaten up so badly that permanent injuries are the result."

"So one of those guys *would* be careful to give his little girl the best treatment if she suffered from XP."

"It's almost as though, by their family loyalty they will somehow erase their guilt over all the lives they have *destroyed.*"

"Paul Giovanni is this godfather's name," Ryan told her.

Miss Stephenson had been holding a nearly full cup of tea. Abruptly her hand shook, and she spilled some of it before putting the cup down on the table, her face suddenly pale.

"What's wrong?" Ryan asked as he saw all the color drain from the Englishwoman's face.

"I know a great deal about Mr. Giovanni," she said. "He was doing business in London before he came to the United States."

"You sound as though there's more to it than that."

She nodded slowly, sadly.

"My brother Derek ran a seafood restaurant near London's famous Soho district. Paul Giovanni demanded protection money. My brother refused. And he—."

She started crying.

Ryan stood and walked around the table to her.

"Twenty years ago that man's goons murdered my brother, Ryan. Derek died in my arms. I . . . I felt so helpless. I wanted to strike back, but I couldn't. I was a Christian, even then. Still, for a long time I carried my hatred with me, without doing anything about it, until the Lord managed to lift that burden from my shoulders."

She looked up at him as he stood by her side.

"Just *hearing* his name, Ryan, the . . . the memories come back in on me. Oh, my young friend, it's so awful to lose a loved one anytime—but *to have him die in that way!*"

He had never seen this side of Miss Stephenson. And now he felt closer to her than ever.

"I know exactly how you feel," he told her.

Her eyes opened wide, and she started to blush.

"Yes!" she exclaimed. "I was so involved in my own tragedy just then that I temporarily forgot that you *do* know what it is to have a loved one torn from you in such a terrible way!"

# Six

Middle-aged, heavy-set Paul Giovanni was sitting in his large den in the beautiful Beverly Hills home he had had designed and built for his family more than ten years earlier. In order to have room for his mansion, Giovanni had spent thousands of dollars to demolish the aging residence of a once-famous movie star.

But that was easily done, for Giovanni had piled up more than enough money over the years. And he was able to buy practically anything he wanted, including a very big private jet, five automobiles, and all the other luxuries he wanted, not to mention a staff of seven full-time servants!

All around him were photographs hanging from the wood-paneled walls, shots of him and political figures, important businessmen, some TV personalities.

*They came to me for favors,* he thought. *They all wanted what I could give them or what they thought I could give them.*

Protection. Money. Power.

*But none of them realized what I would want in return. I smiled and fed them and bought them gifts and made them feel as though they were sitting on top of the world.*

Giovanni stood and walked slowly over to one autographed photo in particular. This one showed him alongside a beautiful blonde-haired movie actress.

*She was so fragile, that sweet, sweet woman. I tried hard to help her. I tried to convince her to stay away from the President of the United States. Being involved in his life was going to be a serious mistake.*

Giovanni sighed deeply. *Too late now, dear friend. There are some things that are beyond even my reach. . . .*

Next he walked back to his desk and picked up a four-by-five snapshot of his daughter Laurene.

*But you, my child, there is never any question of my giving up. I will do whatever it takes to help you. I will finance a hundred clinics if that is what it takes to find a cure. . . .*

He bowed his head and a tear splashed on to his desk. This release of emotions was something that he dared not reveal to the men on his pay-roll. If any of them thought him to be weak, the full extent of his empire might begin to crumble as the whole pack of them started to scramble for pieces of it.

# Seven

**R**yan was talking to a CIA contact on the phone in his bedroom while Chad sat in a chair next to him.

"Yes sir, that's right. I talked to my dad by phone an hour ago. And he said to tell you what my brother and I and our friend saw close to Woodview Rehabilitation Hospital. Since there may be some Mafia connection, he thought we should report it."

Ryan paused.

"Are you sure?" he said into the receiver. "You don't want to hear anything more?"

Ryan listened to what the man at the other end was saying for a couple of minutes longer, then: "Okay, okay, sorry for interfering."

He gulped once, then again as he slowly put the receiver back in its cradle. He was feeling both nervous and a little angry.

"Well, I guess that's it," he said.

"What do you mean?" Chad asked his brother.

"It's hands off. No trespass. Top secret. Whatever you want to call it, we're supposed to forget everything."

"Any explanation?"

"None."

"Chad?"

"Yeah, Ryan?"

"I think it has to do with that Mafia guy."

"Giovanni?"

"I think there's something going on with him."

"What could it be, Ryan?"

"I have no—."

He swung around and faced the computer screen.

"What's going on?" Chad asked.

"I remember an item I spotted a month or so ago, coming through from one of the wire services that Dad has subscribed to. It looked pretty interesting, so I filed it away on my hard disk."

He scrolled through a long list of files, then stopped and flashed the contents of one of them up on the monitor.

"Yes! Here it is."

Chad looked over his shoulder at the information that was just then being transmitted:

It is apparent that ever-increasing numbers of ganglords and their lieutenants are actually going to jail these days. So far, there has been no official explanation from FBI headquarters in Washington, D. C., to account for this unusual recent success record in apprehending these criminals. In the past, mobsters in the United States have usually been able to avoid serving any actual jail time for their various crimes. This was the case with alleged kingpin John Gotti and others whose crimes included the selling of drugs, illegal gambling, gun-running, bribing public officials, and much more. What *is* behind the current situation? For the moment, that seems to be a question without an answer.

The two brothers glanced at one another.

"Bet I know what you're thinking," Chad said.

"Have a go at it, brother."

"You think maybe this Giovanni character has been some kind of undercover agent for the Feds. That's why nothing can be done to upset his operation, in any way. Giovanni's got to remain where he is until he gives his governmental contacts all that he can."

"If he survives, you mean," Ryan added.

"Yeah, and with that rough crowd, nobody can be sure how much longer that will be."

"Guess we better let Barney know what we found out just in case he sees that little girl and the muscle men again," Ryan said. "Who knows what kind of trouble he might get into if he's not warned about this right away?"

"An old guy in a wheelchair? He's not a threat to the mob. What could happen? Be real, will you, Ryan?"

"That's exactly what I'm doing. You know as well as I do that the trouble is . . . well, with Barney, you never know what's going to be happening, you just never know."

# Eight

That night, Barney Fitzsimmons decided he didn't need his wheelchair for a while, and so he left it behind in his room.

Thankfully his therapy had been going along really well.

*I really want to surprise those guys!* he told himself.

Barney was thinking of Ryan and Chad's next visit, for he was determined to show them how strong he had become, how well he could walk.

He told a nurse that he was going to walk outside and get some fresh air. She replied that this would be fine but that he should take his remote alarm with him just in case.

He thanked her, smiling as he raised his hand to show her the little oblong plastic shape he was holding.

"Good for you," she said, smiling back at him.

He reached the main entrance of the hospital and stepped outside, half expecting to see some pale-looking children just beyond the steps, waiting for him. When that wasn't the case, he realized how crazy the notion was.

But he was rewarded with something else.

Just beyond the property line of the hospital was a road, not a major highway by any means, but it was paved at least. In keeping with the secluded location, the road seldom saw very much traffic.

Except that night.

Three cars in a row drove past as he stood and watched.

But not just ordinary ones.

All three were Lincoln Continental stretch limousines, very long, and very black.

*Like something out of a movie,* Barney thought, *some isolated meeting of mobster leaders!*

He was chuckling but then stopped, realizing that he may have hit it exactly right.

*What a chance to trap these guys. With Ryan's and Chad's contacts, we could uncover—.*

He hesitated, knowing that a group of scary men getting together to talk was hardly *evidence* of any federal crime, no matter how suspicious it all appeared to be on the surface.

Barney admitted to himself that his curiosity was easily stirred up.

When he had been on the police force, he was always the one conducting the most successful investigations. His list of arrests was the best on record for the forty years he was on the force.

*I haven't changed a bit,* he told himself. *If only I could—.*

That was when Barney sensed he was being watched. But at first he could see no one.

He held his breath for a few seconds, straining his ears for a sound, a clue that he wasn't imagining anything.

A face.

Like that of the Giovanni child but not entirely the same. If anything, it was even more pale.

It was looking at him through the trees to his left.

He walked off the hospital's front porch and headed toward the pale-faced figure.

As he came closer, he thought the child would turn and run.

Not so.

Whoever it was just stood there, as though waiting for him.

When Barney was within a few feet, he saw how different this one, this young boy, really was.

The skin was more than just pale.

It seemed almost transparent.

He could actually see veins underneath the surface.

And the eyes—!

The boy's eyes were blood-red. It was a sight beyond anything Barney had seen before.

He could also hear brush nearby being trampled underfoot.

"Is someone after you?" he asked. "Do you need help, son?"

The boy, hesitated, then nodded.

"Come with me," Barney said. "We're going inside."

"*NO!*" the little one said, holding his hand in front of his eyes.

Barney looked at him, knowing right away what he meant.

"The light, that's what scares you, isn't it?" he said. "You need to be shielded from it."

The boy nodded sadly.

In back of the two of them, the frantic sounds of pursuit were getting louder, closer.

"Hurry!" Barney said. "Slip under that big bush by the porch. I'll go inside and get someone to help us."

Barney was starting to ache; he was straining his weak muscles too much as he hurried—.

A tough-sounding voice chilled him as it suddenly shouted, "You there, old man! I've come for the kid. Get out of my way."

Abruptly Barney felt himself being knocked to the ground.

He looked up, could see a very broad man grab the little boy and start to walk away with him, not back into the wooded area but toward the road where a car had pulled up and seemed to be waiting.

"No!" Barney screamed. "You can't—."

He managed to get to his feet and stepped in front of them.

"Leave that child alone!" he said as sternly as he could manage through the pain that had taken over his body.

The man stood still for a moment, eying Barney.

"You have no idea what you're talking about," the man said. "Now get out of my way, old man."

"I will *not!*" Barney declared defiantly, in a clear and strong voice. "You leave that little boy alone!"

The man ignored Barney and looked at the little boy.

"Tell us where Laurene is hiding. We must find her," he demanded.

The little boy stubbornly shook his head.

Barney saw this and grabbed ahold of the man's thick wrist. The stranger let go of his grip on the boy as Barney and he wrestled one another to the ground.

Ten years earlier, Barney would have been a match for the other man. But his former injury and time had made him an aging shell of his once top physical form.

Barney screamed in pain and fell to the ground.

The fragile-looking little boy tried to get past Barney's attacker.

But he didn't succeed.

The man grabbed the child again and carried him off toward the awaiting car, which immediately left with them.

Barney was on the ground moaning when two nurses and a doctor came running outside from the hospital.

# Nine

**B**arney's been hurt!

Ryan thanked the doctor who had called from the hospital and then hung up the receiver.

*They don't know all the circumstances, but he's going to be okay....*

Ryan was grateful for that.

*I've got to tell Chad.*

He found his brother in the garage, lifting weights.

For an instant, Ryan paused in the doorway, ashamed of his deep-down feeling of jealousy. He had to admit honestly to himself that, more than once, he had looked at Chad's well-defined muscles and wished that he had spent similar effort in toning his own body.

*Flat stomach, firm biceps, strong legs....*

"Hey, bud, what's happenin'?" Chad said, spotting him.

"It's Barney," Ryan replied.

"What about him?"

"He's been hurt, but he's going to be okay."

Chad put down the barbell he had been lifting.

"Hurt? What happened?"

"There's no way of knowing for sure."

"Nothing?"

"The grass was torn up when they found him."

"A struggle?"

"Might have been."

"Who could be responsible for—?"

Chad cut himself off.

They looked at one another, thinking they knew the answer without ever saying it out loud.

"We need help with this," Chad admitted. "I'm more afraid of a guy like Giovanni than I am of any terrorists."

"Yeah, I know what you mean."

"Our contact at the agency will only tell us that they can't do anything. They'll come up with some excuse like, 'There's no evidence' or something like that."

Ryan agreed with his brother.

"We've gotta talk to Barney."

"Maybe he'll clam up, too."

"I can't picture Barney being scared by anybody's threats."

Ryan was right. He wasn't.

The old guy was a little shaky but not other-wise hurt, except for a couple of sore muscles and a cut on his head from the fall.

"When I was younger . . ." he said wistfully as he sat up in the hospital bed.

"What happens when you tell the staff here the truth?" Ryan asked.

"They act as though it's an old man's craziness," Barney replied. "I even overheard a couple of the nurses talking about how they wish I'd admit that I got a little clumsy, instead of making up some wild fantasy."

"You really think this mobster is involved?" Chad asked. "And the little girl you saw earlier was his daughter?"

"After just being at the receiving end of typical mob behavior, I have less doubt than ever."

"Because of Dad's job we're always supposed to report anything that's the least bit unusual, but when we told our family contact person about this, we were told to forget it. We're getting no coop-eration from anyone," Ryan added.

"Yeah, what can two kids accomplish on their own?" Chad put in.

"If we only had some pictures," said Ryan.

They looked at one another, then at Barney Fitzsimmons.

"That's it!" Chad nearly shouted. "Ryan, remember that great camera Dad gave us two Christmases ago?"

"You bet," Ryan agreed. "Limited production. Highly advanced infrared picture-taking."

"Even at night or in a fog."

"We've never had much of a chance to try it out, Chad."

"Someday we'll have to do just that. The thing wasn't cheap. Dad's gifts should never be wasted," he grinned slyly.

"Yeah, we'll have to try it someday *soon*."

 **Ten**

First Laurene runs off to explore the woods. Then some of the other kids at the clinic decide to enjoy a nighttime adventure in the woods with her. And now an old man gets hurt!" Paul Giovanni was on the thin edge of rage.

He was sitting beside the Olympic-sized pool in his backyard, which itself seemed as big as a football field. Tony Campana, his assistant, had come to him with the news of what had happened.

"I thought that clinic was secure," Giovanni said, his face reddening, hands tightening into fists. "And now it turns out that little children like my daughter can get past all their safeguards. That's not encouraging, Tony, not encouraging at all."

"But we *were* led to believe that those guys did know what they were doing," Campana told him nervously. "Do you want to close it down and move Laurene elsewhere?"

*Laurene!*

*Just the mention of her name quieted him and made him sad at the same time. She had never seen an afternoon sun. She knew only the pale light of a cold moon.*

"I don't know. Let me think about it," Giovanni said sharply. "Now get out of here. Leave me alone, Tony. Do us both a favor, will you? For a change, try to earn the money I pay you."

Campana nodded and went back inside the house.

Giovanni turned his head in the opposite direction. He wanted no one to see the expression on his face.

*Those other kids. . . . They're as bad off as Laurene. . . . Some are even worse. Not all of them have XP. Some are blind. Some have missing arms or legs. Some—.*

The Frankenstein Project.

Giovanni had been told about it a year earlier. And for many of those kids it was their only hope of a cure.

A secret group of doctors had banded together in a common effort to try and find cures to certain diseases and other health problems—especially those affecting children. That in itself was just fine, of course, but it turned out that they were experimenting with new and untested drugs. So the Food and Drug Administration did not formally recognize them. In fact, if too much about their operation was made public, the FDA would have to shut them down.

*When I heard about them, I thought maybe they could help my poor little Laurene.*

He wiped his eyes with the back of his hand.

*But when?* he sighed to himself. *When?*

# Eleven

The little girl was tired.

It seemed to her that she had been tired like that for most of her life. She never saw any daylight. The only time she got to play outside was on nights when there was little of the moon showing in the sky.

Even the full moon was her enemy. But she longed to be able to run and play under its full light, even though it was only a reflection of the sleeping sun's glory. She could somehow pretend to be free at night because it was then that she didn't have to hide in dark places away from the light and people. People would be either frightened when they saw her or, later, perhaps pity her.

Fear—pity.

When Laurene sensed that others loved and cared for her, she responded to them with affection. This was easy to do with her father, when he was away from the cruel-looking men who seemed to be around him all the time.

But mostly she was with strangers—men and women in their white clothes poking at her, sticking her with needles, looking down her throat, peering into her eyes, giving her all kinds of medicine.

Never any different.

It had never been any different, that she could remember. When she was asleep, during the day, she would dream about many things. But she had one favorite fantasy. And, often, while awake at night, she would carry it in her thoughts with the hope that it would come true.

*It would involve a friendly stranger who would come into her sad little life and make her well. One night, she thought she saw who it was at last. This man was old and kindly-looking, and he gently took her hand, more with love, than pity. And he seemed to want to help her, to protect her, to do for her whatever he could.*

*But someone else intruded again, one of those awful men who worked for her father came and grabbed her and took her away.*

Laurene's red-rimmed eyes were opened wide. She could feel cold perspiration all over her.

She sat up in bed, crying. The kind man was real.

It had been no dream that night. This she knew.

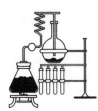 # Twelve

**P**aul Giovanni awoke in the middle of the night, his hand falling instinctively on the empty side of the bed.

*Rose,* he thought. *Dear beloved Rose. . . .*

His wife, Laurene's mother, had suffered from the same condition as their beloved daughter. But she had not developed the disease until just before their daughter was born. Then several years later, a rival mob kidnapped Rose, killing her two bodyguards.

The next day, despite her pleas, she was forced out into the bright sunlight.

Rose died in great pain. And yet she did so with great dignity, he had found out a short while later.

*My wife stood tall, proud for as long as she could. I am told that she was even smiling some, until the very last, when she had to drop to the ground. Some thought she might have been praying during the final moments because they heard her say the words, "Father, forgive them. Please, dearest Lord, forgive them. "*

After her death, Paul Giovanni had begun a large-scale war of vengeance against those responsible for the murder.

Violence.

A great deal of it.

It was a time of extreme violence all along the West Coast, from the Baja Peninsula to Washington State. It lasted a total of more than six months as Giovanni struck back at the rival gangsters.

*Like Chicago, when Al Capone was top dog,* Giovanni thought. *But I had to do what I did. I had no other choice.*

Eventually the survivors in the other gang (and there weren't many after Giovanni was done with them) went into hiding. They thought he didn't know where they were, but he did. Yet he had decided to leave the rest of them alone, at least as long as they "behaved" themselves.

Giovanni became the most powerful mobster west of the Rockies.

*I have great power,* he told himself as he had done countless moments over the years. *It is true that I can order the execution of anyone who happens to displease me. Yet I can't bring Rose back, and I can't get a cure for Laurene. What does all the rest mean?*

He looked at the photograph of his wife beside his bed. It had been taken inside the church on their wedding day. She was so beautiful, with thin porcelain-like cheeks and delicate little lips. Neither of them had any idea then that she had the dreaded XP.

*Religion was always important to her. She talked a lot about salvation,* Giovanni remembered. *I told her that the only salvation for me was having more guns than the next guy, bribing more officials and having more bodyguards.*

Yet, as Giovanni's eyes surveyed that photo for the thousandth time, he knew that, despite her awful condition, Rose had lived her short life with a peace that he had never been able to claim as his own.

*She kept talking about religion, about a Comforter who had been sent to be with her every step of the way.*

He fell back on the bed, closed his eyes. He was beginning to understand.

"If only. . . ." he whispered out loud in the darkness.

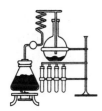

# Thirteen

The locket!" Ryan was saying. "If we're caught, we can say that we were on the grounds of the hospital because we wanted to return the locket to its owner. What could be more ordinary than that?"

"At night?" Chad said skeptically.

Ryan scratched the top of his head, realizing that his brother had seen the problem with that course of action right away.

"Yeah, you're right," he said. "But we have the camera, and it's no good during the day. What do we do then?"

"I wasn't saying we should cancel what we've planned, Ryan. It's just that we shouldn't fool ourselves that the locket will help us all that much. We go ahead at night. We get some photos. And maybe we can embarrass authorities into investigating. If the locket helps, that's great. But we can't expect too much. I know we can't sit back and just wonder about what's going on!"

They had been in dangerous situations a number of times. This one didn't seem any worse than some of the others. After all, even gangsters wouldn't just mow down a couple of kids!

"If we're careful enough, we can get what we want, without being spotted," Chad added. "But, first, we've got to find the place somehow and get an idea of what it looks like. There must be a clinic or something close to Woodview Hospital, probably on the other side of that wooded area. We need to know as much as possible what the layout is before we start tiptoeing around in it."

"Saturday," Ryan said. "We could go in another direction and drive by there on the way to see Barney."

"That's a plan!" his brother agreed.


Ryan decided to spend some time at home after school, rather than getting involved in any student activities, as he sometimes did. Chad stayed for more wrestling practice. He was rapidly becoming the school's top wrestler, and he needed to stay in training.

Ryan had a wealth of reference works on a CD-ROM disk as well as through computer research services. After finding nothing on the disk, he decided to go through the research services. One of them actually had available something called the *Annals of Crime.*

He saw listings of information on Al Capone, Bugsy Siegel, Frank Nitti, and many more.

*More criminals than heroes!* he thought, saddened by that fact. *The bad guys seem to get greater media attention.*

Finally—

*Paul Giovanni!*

He learned when Giovanni was born and where. . . .

*In Sicily . . . in the worst area of poverty in that region . . . was said to have made a vow that whatever family he started would never find themselves in similar awful conditions.*

Ryan leaned back in his chair, realizing that he was beginning to feel some sympathy for this man. . . . *born into poverty . . . wife dead . . . daughter afflicted by a terrible disease . . . probably people ready to murder him given the slightest opportunity.*

But then Ryan knew who he was dealing with in the final analysis, someone who was willing to use blackmail, bribery, injury, murder, and whatever else he could think of to get whatever he wanted.

Yet, according to what he had just read, there were people who genuinely did seem to *love* Paul Giovanni. They pledged absolute loyalty to him.

How could that be?

Did anyone *love* Hitler? Or did they simply want power? After all, almost all his followers had deserted him like rats from a doomed ship when it was clear that his cause had gone down in defeat.

Ryan couldn't imagine Stalin, Idi Amin, or any of the other dictators/criminals being loved. Yet mobster Paul Giovanni seemed to have earned that love, according to the reports that were coming through on the computer.

# Fourteen

**R**yan waited until his brother had returned home from another wrestling practice at school.

"Chad, I think there is some other place we need to go before we try to find where those kids come from," he said clumsily.

Chad was munching on an apple as they stood in the kitchen.

"What are you thinking of, Ryan?"

"Giovanni's neighborhood."

Chad nearly dropped the apple.

"*What*?" he said. "Are you—?"

"—going crazy!" Ryan interrupted. "If we can somehow make contact with Giovanni, we—."

Chad continued looking at Ryan as though his brother had completely flipped out.

"What would that prove?"

"He might let us see what's going on."

"What reason would he have? It's nonsense, Ryan."

Chad threw up his hands in unbelief.

"Use that brain power of yours. Think about what you've said. There's a lot of danger, and very little good that could come of it. Get real, will you?"

Ryan didn't sleep well. His attention was all wrapped up with a mobster and a pale-faced, fragile-looking little girl. There was no way he could just let go of thinking about them.

It was about 2:30 A.M. when he got out of bed and onto his knees.

"Lord," he prayed, "is this idea foolish? If it is, then help me to drop it and never turn back to it again. If not, I need to feel at peace, Lord. I need to feel that it's an idea that You—and You alone— guided into my head somehow. And I need Your protection, for it'll be as though I'm going into the Valley of the Shadow of Death. . . . Amen."

Ryan climbed back into bed and lay there for a few minutes, his eyes open, his mind at full speed, thinking of a certain little section of Los Angeles known as Little Italy.

*They love this Paul Giovanni. They come close to thinking that God sent him in answer to prayer. How could that be?*

There would be no answers until two days later, on Saturday, when Chad and he took a drive into the city and—.

*Oh, man,* Ryan thought, with more than a little uncertainty. *That's if I can convince Chad to go along with me!*

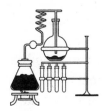

# Fifteen

In the morning, as it turned out, Ryan didn't have any convincing to do.

"You left your computer on last night," Chad said between mouthfuls of raisin flake cereal.

"Not again!" Ryan reacted. "I was really tired. Guess I just got careless."

"I didn't want to mess with it so I left it on."

Ryan was starting to get up from the chair and hurry to his bedroom.

"I read on the monitor some of the stuff you dug up about Giovanni," Chad told him.

"What do you think?"

"Pretty fascinating. He's a strange man. He has a good side and an evil one, that's for sure."

"Two natures. But doesn't everyone have a good side and a bad side?"

"That's right. But in Giovanni those natures are somehow more extreme than with most people. He's made that area he controls as safe as though

**61**

it had FBI agents at every corner. He's supporting several charities all by himself."

"And he's sponsoring an entire clinic just so his daughter can get the proper treatment!"

"Amazing," Chad had to admit. "He's a wicked man, for sure, but he's not completely down the drain."

"Just what I was thinking," Ryan replied.

"I wonder if he could be reached for Christ."

Ryan sat back down on the chair.

"I wonder. . . ."

"Wonder what?"

"If he's already accepted Christ into his life."

"How could he and remain a Mafia leader?"

"Maybe Giovanni wants out. Maybe that's why he's cooperating with the authorities."

Chad was about to laugh at that notion when he stopped and considered it, biting on his lower lip as he did so.

"I wonder how close you are to the truth, Ryan?"

"Are we on for Saturday?"

Chad looked across the table at Ryan.

"Nothin' could stop me now!" he said, glad he could make his younger brother happy.

"Great!" Ryan replied, admitting to himself that he had a pretty sensible older brother after all.

# Sixteen

Tony Campana had worked as bodyguard / errand boy for Paul Giovanni for almost five years.

*Giovanni, you're the worst, the worst,* Campana told himself. *A fat, arrogant toad! I don't care if you're the godfather or not.*

He was fed up.

Campana stood at the full length mirror in his apartment. His shirt off, his biceps flexed, he thought, *Giovanni, you assume I'm nothing more than a muscle-bound moron, able to do what you decide but nothing more.*

He started chuckling.

*A stupid man couldn't be planning what I've had in the works for weeks now. Paul Giovanni, you'll be very sorry that you ever offended me. I regret only that I didn't start something before now.*

Campana walked over to a round table and picked up the snub-nosed revolver on top. Then he turned around and shot at the mirror, which ended up in countless thousands of pieces at his feet.

*Soon,* he thought, *soon you'll realize just what I really am capable of, Paul Giovanni!*

He looked at the shattered glass and continued chuckling.

Little Italy seemed to be just what its name implied, a miniature version of the country itself.

Pizza shops. Bakeries. A general store. A Roman Catholic church. Street vendors offering vegetables and fruits. And row after row of apartments.

Plus many restaurants and clubs.

One of these was called, simply, The Place.

It was where Paul Giovanni conducted much of his mob business. His private court was in a back-room office.

Ryan had found out about it through his computer sources. Chad and he went to Little Italy that Saturday with a definite plan.

They traveled all over the neighborhood asking questions about Giovanni. They suspected that someone eventually would search them out and drag the two of them to see Giovanni. Surely he would want to know what they were up to. If they were just to walk up to the entrance to The Place, they wouldn't be allowed to see him under any circumstances.

And it worked out just as they planned. But before it did, they got a clear picture of what this man meant to the neighborhood called Little Italy.

"He's wonderful," a plump old woman said as she looked up from the stand where she was selling heads of lettuce. "Because of Paul Giovanni, we can walk the streets at night."

"But he does this by the same violence that he's made you safe from," Ryan pointed out bravely.

"Who cares?" she said, throwing up her hands. "I just know I don't have to be worried about being mugged by some hooligans!"

They found the same attitude evident among just about everyone else in that section of Los Angeles. This included a middle-aged man who was sitting on the steps leading up to the entrance of the duplex where he lived on the top floor.

"One of my daughters was attacked years ago, before Paul Giovanni took over," he told them. "Today that would never happen."

"Out of fear," Chad remarked.

"But it's the street gangs who fear *us* now because of that man. I'd rather *them* be afraid, kid. Now get out of here!"

A few minutes later, Ryan turned to his brother and said, "You know, it's strange, but they all seem so happy around here."

"The problem is that there may be no drug selling going on in the streets, but it's happening behind closed doors at The Place, you can bet on that."

"You're right, Chad. *Their* kids aren't going down the drain, but what about other kids in other neighborhoods?"

A black sedan pulled up to the curb as they stood on the sidewalk, talking.

Two very big men hopped out.

"In the car!" one of them shouted.

"Why, what's wrong?" Chad asked, pretending surprise and fear.

"You'll find out. *Now get in!*"

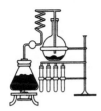

# Seventeen

**R**yan and Chad were almost dragged through the smoke-filled bar area of The Place, and into a room in the back.

Paul Giovanni was sitting in an oversized leather chair.

"You've been asking a lot of questions in my neighborhood, kids," he growled, "a lot of questions about me. Now what's going on?"

Both brothers froze at first.

"You got mouths," Giovanni added. "You've been using them all over the street. I can have one of my guys here pry open your jaws and knock a few teeth out in the process if that will help!"

Ryan's eyes widened.

"Sir, we're . . . we're real . . . sorry about interfering," he stuttered. "It has to do with your daughter."

Giovanni's face remained as cold and hard as earlier.

"What about Laurene?"

"Could we talk to you alone?" Chad asked.

Giovanni paused, narrowing his eyes as he looked at the two of them. Then he told both men to leave.

"Talk," he said when they were gone.

"Mr. Giovanni, we know about—," Ryan started to say.

Chad brought a finger up to his lips, indicating that his brother shouldn't say anything.

"Hey, what gives with you?" Giovanni said, frowning.

Chad pointed to a pad of paper on top of the battered old desk behind which the man was sitting.

Giovanni nodded, handing it to him along with a pencil. Chad wrote something on the top sheet and then slid the pad across the desk toward Giovanni.

*One of those men slipped a bug under the lampshade on that table next to the door.*

"What in the—?" Giovanni started to say, then stopped. The look on their faces told him that they weren't play-acting or that this wasn't some sort of crazy teenage prank.

He tore off the sheet Chad had written on, and scrawled something on the next one with a ballpoint pen he retrieved from the center drawer of the desk.

*How come you were able to spot that, kid?*

Chad took the pad and added another message:

*Our father's in a line of business that he's taught us a lot about, sir. That's all I can say. . . .*

Giovanni nodded and stuffed the written-on sheets of paper in his trouser pocket.

"Hey, guys," he said, "it's a little warm in here. Bet you could use some fresh air. You there look pretty hardy but your skinny little brother's all pale-looking."

*Thanks, mister!* Ryan said to himself. *Thanks a lot!*

Giovanni stood and pointed to a door to their left.

They nodded and followed him as he went outside. They found themselves standing in a very narrow alley.

"No ears here," he said. "Now, what's this all about?"

Ryan told him about his experience, and then Chad related Barney Fitzsimmons' own encounters.

Giovanni leaned back against the left wall of the alley.

"It never ends," he whispered.

"Sir?" Ryan asked. "Are you a Christian?"

Giovanni turned sharply toward Ryan.

"What makes you ask that?" he said.

"It's just a hunch, sir. Are you?" Ryan persisted, knowing that he could be on very dangerous ground if the man was at all antagonistic toward anyone who happened to be "religious."

Giovanni looked at him, a slight smile curling up the corners of his mouth.

The answer to that question surprised Ryan and Chad.

"Yes . . . I am, but it's something new for me."

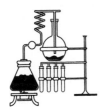

# Eighteen

**P**aul Giovanni sat in the back of the black, stretch limousine with Ryan and Chad. He had assured them that his driver could be trusted, but still he asked that the sound-proofing window between the front and back seats be rolled up anyway, for maximum privacy.

"The Frankenstein Project is making all kinds of medical breakthroughs. But these discoveries have to be kept secret until thorough testing can be done. This project happens to be run by a certain government agency," he said. "They furnished all the doctors and other members of the staff. That was the deal."

Ryan and Chad could hardly speak.

"You both are so quiet all of a sudden," Giovanni observed warmly. "Have I shocked you?"

It was Ryan who spoke first.

"I don't think *shocked* is the word, sir. *Surprised* is more like it."

"You had guessed anything but what I've just told you, is that it?"

Ryan nodded.

"I figured I could accomplish two worthwhile purposes," Giovanni continued. "First, I could get my daughter treatment that might not have been possible otherwise, not because the cost was beyond my reach, but because my contacts go only so far. Second, by spilling the beans on whatever I knew about *mafioso* activities . . . well, I could somehow make up for a lot of the terrible wrongs I've done in the past."

Ryan and Chad were silent again.

Giovanni looked at them and continued.

"I realize that forgiveness and cleansing for the Christian are based on faith in Christ as Savior and Lord. But that's not what I'm talking about. I want my mind clear as well as my emotions," Giovanni said, tapping his forehead and his chest. "I've been doing such terrible things for so many years that—."

He stopped talking for a moment, emotions choking off the words.

Ryan felt sorry for Giovanni. He knew that the man was taking greater risks because of his walk in Christ than most Christians would ever find necessary.

"I find the Frankenstein Project to be one of the most eye-opening involvements I've had in a lifetime," Giovanni went on to say. "What I saw under one roof made me realize how much people suffer because of what others have done."

"I don't understand, sir," Chad admitted.

"You'll see. There are youngsters who are, in many cases, suffering for what selfish, unthinking parents have done."

"Like drinking alcohol during pregnancy?" Ryan remarked.

"Exactly that! But more. There are cases where a parent was drunk and the family car went out of control, and the child, a passenger, was paralyzed for life or lost an arm or a leg. And if it's not alcohol, it's drugs."

They decided to tell him about their mother's death without saying too much about their father's job. After all, it had been in all the papers.

"We know about innocent people being hurt," Ryan commented. "Our mother died in an explosion because some terrorists were trying to get at our father."

"Oh . . ." Giovanni said, his tone changing ever so slightly. "What were the circumstances?"

"A bomb. She got in our car, and it went off."

"How long ago was that, Ryan?" Giovanni asked, sounding as though he had to force the words out.

"A little over three years ago."

"In Los Angeles somewhere?"

"Not in the city itself. It was at our home in the San Fernando Valley, just beyond the Laurel Canyon Pass."

"I see," he replied. "Sorry to hear about that."

Ryan and Chad glanced at one another.

Paul Giovanni's voice had been trembling just then, and neither of them had any idea why that was so.

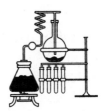# Nineteen

**N**o way. . . .

There was no way Ryan and Chad could have predicted a week earlier what was going to happen.

Certainly not that they would be standing before a special one-way viewing window watching an amazing ten-year-old boy in the next room.

"He had lost all his fingers due to an automobile accident," Dr. Adrian Cosmatos told them. "Now look!"

The youngster had a new set of fingers and was learning to play the piano. He was doing very well in the early stages.

"They're artificial, of course," Dr. Cosmatos told them, "but we just may be on the verge of something else."

"Limb regeneration," Ryan spoke up. "It used to be only something out of a science fiction story. Guess that's why it's called the Frankenstein Project."

The doctor turned to him.

"That's very good, young man," he said, more than a little impressed. "How did you know?"

"Sir, I have a heavy-duty bunch of information services linked in with my computer at home."

"He's also skipped a grade in school," Chad put in.

"Skipped a—?" Dr. Cosmatos started to say, then stopped. "Perhaps you should be working here for us."

"I'd like that!" Ryan told him, a broad smile on his face.

They saw a number of other children, different groups with different conditions or diseases: Boys and girls who had been blinded could now see due to special new treatments. Others with cancer were on the way to being cured. Those with leukemia were experiencing remarkable recoveries.

"It's like a dream," Ryan remarked.

"A wonderful dream," Paul Giovanni said.

Ryan and Chad looked at the man, amazed at the remarkable medical breakthroughs he was finding. They could only imagine what he had been like before he accepted Christ into his life. If the reports were true, he would have made the worst gangsters of the 1920s look sparkling clean in comparison.

But now . . .

And then they came to the XP ward.

It was unnerving for them to see so many of these youngsters together in one setting. And the setting itself was quite strange.

It was a playroom in which heavy black curtains had been drawn across the two small windows. The windows themselves had also been painted black so the children could not accidently expose themselves to sunlight.

The only light came from a group of specially-placed candles.

Dr. Cosmatos explained that the children also got to play outside at night when conditions were just right. "But this presents another problem," he said. "These children want so much to be like other children that sometimes they try to hide and wait for the sun to come up."

"How can they stand it?" Ryan whispered.

"It is either that or die, my friend," Giovanni told him. "It was even worse with Laurene's mother."

"But you married her even so," Chad remarked, with an admiration for the man that was growing by the minute.

"At first Rose did not know she had inherited the disease. She was an orphan and did not know her parents. Then when Laurene was born, she discovered it had been developing for years, but very, very slowly. But that was another problem.

She had been so active before she was forced into her new lifestyle that it was hard for her to give up something as simple as spending a day at the beach."

*. . . a day at the beach.*

Ryan and Chad went to Malibu Beach often, getting there by traveling along Pacific Coast Highway. Both of them surfed, but Chad was far better at the sport. His muscular body gave him more athletic control. And it was always Chad who had girls flocking around him, leaving Ryan to wander off on his own.

*I can't imagine what it would be like not to be able to spend summer afternoons riding some waves,* Ryan thought.

"At least children born with XP symptoms," Giovanni continued, "never get accustomed to a normal lifestyle. For them, living at night, staying away from bright lights, never getting out in the sun are life as usual. They've never known anything else."

"Your wife was different though?" Chad asked.

"Yes, she was. For her, the symptoms didn't appear at all early in her life. Then, just before Laurene was born, she began to get sores on her exposed arms and face that took a great deal of time to heal. And, later, new ones didn't really heal at all."

"And you think, by studying your wife's case

history, that you'll get some clue, unknown right now, as to why her system was able to hold XP dormant for so long?" Ryan suggested.

"You've done it again, young man!" Giovanni exclaimed. "I can see why you've advanced so quickly in school."

Ryan blushed, but, in fact, he was used to remarks like that one. He was one of a kind, as the expression goes. The high school that Chad and he attended was filled with teachers and administrators who were amazed at the progress Ryan was making in his classes.

"I never had a son of my own," Giovanni added, "but if I had, I'd have prayed every night that he was like the two of you. I see two brothers who genuinely love one another and who have managed to survive an awful tragedy of their own. You two are as self-sufficient as any young people I've ever met."

"Responsibility is something Mom always insisted we learn," Chad said. "Guess it's a good thing with Dad away so much."

Dr. Cosmatos repeated something he'd mentioned a short while earlier, but this time with much more seriousness.

"Your abilities could be very useful to us here, at some point," he said. "Would you consider helping us?"

"Like *Doogie Howser?*" Ryan said, referring to

a television series about a teenage surgeon.

"Well, yes, sort of. However, that's often fantasy. What I'm talking about here is real."

Ryan smiled.

"Let's talk about it sometime," he replied. The possibility of using whatever intelligence God had given him to help out afflicted children was very appealing.

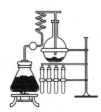

# Twenty

I became what I was out of necessity," Paul Giovanni was saying as the four of them all sat in Dr. Cosmatos' private office.

"But the man who makes possible all of this wonderful work to help sick children couldn't be even close to the same one who used to order the execution of anyone who threatened him," the doctor added.

"People do change when they accept Christ into their lives," Ryan remarked. "We've seen it again and again. So has Dad. It changes the center of interest in their life and adds a whole new outlook."

"That's true," Giovanni agreed. "But there was a problem at first. Before, I never felt guilty about all the hurt and heartache I was responsible for. But once I *really* knew about Christ, I saw so clearly what I had done. I wanted to die. I couldn't face each morning without the most awful depression, a kind of deep, deep sadness."

*. . . the most awful depression.*

Even though they had never experienced the extreme guilt of this man, Ryan and Chad knew what depression was like. It happened to both of them after their mother died. Not having her around would have been bad enough if she had died from some disease or in an accident. But the tragic way she died—that made their sorrow much worse. Nothing had been able to take their minds off what had happened.

"How did you keep all this from the men around you?" Chad asked.

"I didn't lose that part of my self-control," Giovanni replied. "What it amounts to is that I just drain myself of all emotions when others are around. That way they can't detect how I actually do feel!"

Again Paul Giovanni spoke to them from his very heart! They knew that because they, too, had tried to drain themselves of all emotion after their mother's death.

"You understand, don't you?" Giovanni said, his eyes filling with tears.

"We do, sir," Ryan assured him. "When Mom died, we had guilt, too. We couldn't help thinking if only we all had been more careful . . . if only there was some routine about checking the car every morning to see whether it had been tampered with or not. We just never imagined anyone being so cruel as to get at Dad through any of us!"

Giovanni looked at his new young friends and smiled slightly, a smile of appreciation and affection.

"If evil is on someone's mind, if it stays there for weeks or months or longer, then it can lead to all kinds of violent, terrible acts, Ryan. Believe me, I know."

Ryan felt a chill as he repeated in his mind those four words spoken so solemnly by this man with such a dark and haunting past.

. . . *believe me, I know.*


Tony Campana rejoiced when he learned that Giovanni had gone on a sudden trip to the clinic.

*We'll get him there. He won't risk anything with his daughter and all those other kids around!*

"We grab him and then dump that massive frame of his in some isolated canyon deep in the Santa Monica Mountains," he told Giorgio Armelli, a short, weaselly little man.

There would be no more orders from Giovanni. By the next morning, he, Tony Campana, would be giving orders of his own.

Armelli handed him a sheet of paper.

"This might interest you," he said.

Campana unfolded it and read the contents.

"Ryan and Chad Bartlett, sons of Andrew Bartlett. Mother died in car bomb explosion attributed to Middle Eastern terrorists."

He paused, then repeated their names: "Ryan and Chad Bartlett!"

Campana snapped his fingers, as though suddenly realizing something that had been half-forgotten. Then he hurriedly finished reading the rest of what was written on that sheet and crumpled it up into a ball.

"What will those kids do when they find out it wasn't terrorists at all?" Campana said. "Maybe they'll want to pull the trigger themselves after we get ahold of Giovanni, *the man who ordered the car bomb that killed their mother!*"

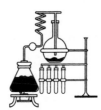# Twenty-one

**L**aurene Giovanni was very intelligent but also shy.

"She would have a great many possibilities ahead of her in life if it weren't for XP." Dr. Cosmatos told them this before they entered the eight-year-old's room at the clinic.

He was obviously saddened by what he saw in Laurene's future.

"Dr. Cosmatos is having great difficulty saying what I've had to live with for so long," Giovanni added. "Those who suffer from XP have weakened immune systems, and they are prone to skin and eye cancers. Many XP patients end up being blind, if they live much past their teens."

"Blind and dying," Chad said softly.

"Some would say that I should be very, very angry with God because of my wife's condition and her death, and now the way Laurene has to live. But I don't feel that way. Sure their disease causes me great sadness. I would even have taken their place in all the suffering if I could. But there is something else. These tragedies in my own life remind me all too well of the sorrow I've caused countless others. Over the years I caused many families to suffer simply because one of their members seemed somehow to be getting in my way at a given moment."

Ryan and Chad saw the way he had been looking at them just then, and they wondered what the expression on his face meant.

Paul Giovanni and Dr. Cosmatos were sitting on the lawn outside the clinic, with Ryan and Chad.

"I've known Paul for only a year or so," the doctor was saying. "But I continue to be more and more impressed with him, you know. He's displaying a lot of courage by doing what he's doing."

Giovanni winced at that.

"No commercials, please," he said, holding up his hand, but chuckling at the same time. "It's good to have people around me who I know I can trust. You're as much a blessing to me as I could ever hope for."

Ryan noted the use of the word *blessing,* not exactly the sort of thing he'd expect a 300-pound *mafioso* don to be saying.

"You really are dedicated to your new faith," Ryan observed out loud, an expression of appreciation on his face.

"Totally," Giovanni said.

"Even though it means taking your life in your hands," Chad added, "and opening yourself up to all kinds of danger?"

"That's the least I can do."

He closed his hands tightly together into a single, big fist.

"And that's what I did in the past, squashing them like they were bugs of one sort or another."

He released his hands and waved an arm in the direction of the clinic.

"Quite a few of those children are orphans," he said, "their parents gone because of me."

He looked at both of them.

"I guess I can't escape the guilt I feel," he added, "and I wonder if—."

His words were drowned out by the *screech* of tires on the road directly in front of them.

Half a dozen men jumped out of two separate cars. Each was holding a revolver except for one who had a machine gun.

"Some things never change," Giovanni whispered.

He seemed not at all surprised.

"Every Mafia godfather suspects something like this will happen at some point in his rule, my friends."

He was too big to run very quickly, and so he didn't even bother to get to his feet as the others approached.

The men formed a circle around Giovanni, Dr. Cosmatos, Ryan, and Chad.

"Who's behind this?" Giovanni asked.

No one answered.

"As soon as Campana finds out, he'll go on the warpath, you know."

Just then, another sedan pulled up behind the other two cars.

Giovanni's mouth dropped open as he saw Tony Campana get out and walk toward them.

He managed to scramble to his feet and lunge at his once-trusted aide. The man with the machine gun hit him on the side of his head with its hard butt. He fell to the ground, dazed.

"Why, Tony?" Giovanni mumbled, his voice streaked with pain. "Why are you doing this?"

"Ah, it was all right for you to muscle out your predecessor," Campana replied, his voice cold, "but somehow you're surprised if I do the same thing with you. Hypocritical, wouldn't you say, Paul?"

Campana then turned to Ryan and Chad, who were looking at him with apprehension.

"But it's not the worst example of that sort of thing, Paul, is it?" Campana said, sneering.

"Don't," Giovanni interrupted. "Leave it alone. You're getting what you want. Don't do this, Tony, don't—!"

"But you have nothing to say about such things anymore," Campana reminded him. "This is no longer your ball game, as the expression goes."

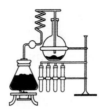

# Twenty-Two

**M**idnight.

Long hours had passed with no communication whatever from their captors. The entire clinic staff, along with Dr. Cosmatos, Paul Giovanni, Ryan, and Chad, had been locked in the dining hall and told nothing. Now they nervously waited in this large room in which the patients and staffers usually ate together three times a day.

"Some of the kids need constant medical attention," Dr. Cosmatos worried out loud. "There has got to be some way that these hoodlums can be appealed to, reasoned with—there *must* be!"

He turned and looked apologetically at Giovanni right after he had used the word *hoodlums*.

"I'm sorry, Paul," he started to say. "I just feel so—."

"It's the right word," Giovanni interrupted him. "I have *been* a hoodlum for just about all my life."

"You mean all your adult life, don't you?" Ryan asked, sure that the man had exaggerated a bit.

"No, it's been longer than that. I learned how to steal back in the streets of Sicily and Rome where I took things from tourists and fruit vendors and shop owners. I grabbed my first purse when I was five years old."

Giovanni seemed amused by the startled expressions on Ryan's and Chad's face.

"But then that's not unusual, you know. In Harlem, kids do the same thing. In Los Angeles, there are poor parents who look the other way when their youngsters are bringing home 'gifts'— gifts of food, money, and other items.

"Yet it's not only the poor, although among such families, stealing *becomes* something of a way of life, you know. All anyone has to do is look at the news stories of all those middle class teenagers who are caught stealing. Some do it in order to finance their drug habits. Others do it just for kicks, a wild flurry of thefts just to impress their friends. How many are there who are committing crimes and are not apprehended by the police? The number must be huge!

"There is one big difference between the Paul Giovanni of those days and what happens today. None of those kids in the crime scene now will ever be anything but rotten little delinquents— in jail, out of jail, in jail, out of jail, and then maybe dying in some gutter or an abandoned building because of the way their bodies have been wasted by drugs.

"I went beyond all that, you know. I eventually got a group of expensive lawyers in double-breasted suits and foreign sports cars to keep me out of prison. Pay some lawyers a lot of money and you can buy anything they have, their brains, their experience, even their souls."

"But not loyalty," Dr. Cosmatos observed. "Not even from those men who have been at your side for such a long time. They become modern Judases all too easily, I'm afraid . . . betrayers."

"Nor can you buy freedom from constant pain for an innocent little girl," Giovanni added sadly, "not even that."

He started pacing the floor.

"I've avoided prison all these years, but Laurene lives in her own kind of prison. And her mother was executed by my enemies. They—."

He stopped abruptly, his eyes darting from side to side.

"Why haven't they done something with me by now?" he asked. "What are they waiting for?"

Ryan was on the same wavelength.

"Are you thinking, sir, that they're waiting until the sun is overhead and then—," he said, but couldn't finish because the thought was too terrible.

*"Yes!"* Giovanni shouted, his face wet with perspiration. "That's exactly what I think is going to happen. They're going to do the same horrible thing to Laurene that others of their kind did to my wife Rose."

His face twisted into deep wrinkles at the thought. *"Only this time they're going to force me to watch!"*

# Twenty-three

*P*aul Giovanni was wrong.

*Campana and his partners didn't plan to wait until noon the next day. They had something else in mind.*

*And it was to happen an hour past midnight.*

Some members of the staff at the clinic had managed to fall asleep. But Ryan and Chad could not, and Giovanni and Dr. Cosmatos dozed off only fitfully.

"We've got to get in touch with someone," Chad whispered to Ryan.

"If we could only sneak out of here and use a phone somewhere."

"They may have done something with the communications inside the clinic," Chad pointed out. "We could do some crazy stuff to get to a phone and then find that it wasn't working."

"Yes, but not the car phone in Giovanni's limo!" Ryan pointed out, his tone triumphant. "That probably would not occur to them. And I think we can count on Giovanni having a set of keys to the car itself."

Chad threw his head back and almost shouted his appreciation of his brother's "smarts," but stopped as he looked around at those asleep in the large room.

"Let's tell Giovanni," he said.

"But how do we get to the car?"

Chad smiled, as he pointed upward.

"Ask for the Lord's help?" Ryan asked, then agreed. "Of course, but—."

"*This* time I meant something a little different," Chad interrupted.

Ryan looked up at the ceiling.

"The air-conditioning ducts!" he said. "Of course. And it's got to be me since you or anyone else here is too big to fit inside."

"I hate that part of it, Ryan. There's a lot of risk involved."

"We don't know that they're not going to kill some of us anyway. Giovanni's on the list. Probably Laurene, as cruel and dirty as that sounds. They wouldn't necessarily stop there."

Both of them walked over to the opposite end of the room, where Paul Giovanni and the doctor were sitting. They told them what they had in mind. The two men nodded as they were talking.

"Great idea," Giovanni admitted without hesitation. "We don't have other options, and that sounds like it might work."

He paused, looking first at Ryan, then at Chad.

"I . . . I have something to tell you," he said.

"It can wait," Ryan replied. "We've got to move fast."

"You may not be very interested in doing anything to help Laurene or me when you hear me out."

"Sir," Ryan persisted, "if we don't get help, it's possible that *none* of us may get out of this place except as bodies on stretchers."

Giovanni hesitated, then admitted that Ryan was right, and postponed what he was going to say.

The staffers were awakened, and everybody pitched in to help. They formed a flesh-and-blood totem pole that reached to the relatively low ceiling where the grill to the cooling system vent was easy to loosen and set aside.

"Pray for me, everyone!" Ryan said as he crawled into the air-conditioning duct. Slowly he made his way along the aluminum "tunnels" that were located throughout the building. Dr. Cosmatos had drawn a diagram for him, and he prayed that it was accurate enough for him to get to a duct close to an outside door.

Ryan was small and skinny, and his lack of extra pounds served him well. Perhaps five minutes or so later, he decided that he was halfway along on his odd little journey. He was just starting past several vent openings like the one he had entered from the dining hall.

Voices.

He recognized one of these.

Tony Campana's.

Ryan stopped and peered around the frame of the duct, looking through the metal slots placed over it.

"It's beautiful," Campana was saying. "I can't believe how well this is going to work out."

Ryan was about to scoot on past when he heard something that stopped him cold.

"It's amazing that we have Andrew Bartlett's kids here," the man with Campana stated.

"Don't I know it!"

Ryan froze.

*. . . we have Andrew Bartlett's kids here.*

Those words fairly shouted themselves through Ryan's mind.

*Dad! Why are they mentioning Dad? What could they possibly know about him? And— and—.*

"We had to lay low after blowing up his wife like that," Campana continued. "Paul was never crazy about the idea, you know. He hated involving innocent people. He kept saying that that just wasn't our style. But I managed to convince him that Bartlett was getting too close to us because of our Middle East gun-running connections.

"If we couldn't reach the man himself, we had to send a message some other way through harming his wife or kids. We had to tell him to lay off. But Bartlett didn't pay attention. We just succeeded in making him mad. Too bad for the terrorists. And lucky for us he never discovered our connection with them. Besides, the Bartlett woman's death caused so much of a stink among *our* people that *we* were almost shot as punishment."

"In addition to everything else, Bartlett or some other Fed somehow must have gotten to Paul, and I'm certain," the other man said.

"—that Paul betrayed some of our Mafia brothers. The lousy fourflusher!"

"Doesn't matter much, does it, Tony? We eliminate Giovanni, blame it on the Feds, and *we* become the brotherhood's new leaders on the West Coast. Your plan is the best, Tony, the best!"

"Yeah, yeah, stop buttering me up."

"But it's true. Before we made it look like the car bomb had been placed by Middle Eastern terrorists—and *this* time, the Feds are the bad guys. *Great stuff!*"

Ryan was so startled by what he had heard just then that he lost his balance and fell back against the side of the aluminum air-conditioning duct, making some noise in the process. The two spun around, not certain of what had happened or the direction of the sound.

"What the—?" Campana said, whipping out his revolver, the other man doing the same.

They rushed out of the room in which they had been standing, and both looked frantically up and down the corridor.

"Were we hearing things?" Campana asked stupidly.

"Hardly, but whoever it was disappeared fast! Probably one of the kids they treat here, Tony."

"I hope so, my friend. *Nothing* can be allowed to stop what we're doing here. *Nothing!*"

# Twenty-four

*O*h, *Lord, please, see my brother Ryan through this!* Chad was praying to himself. *See us all through the next few hours, dear Jesus, and may Your name be honored and glorified.*

He felt a hand on his shoulder.

Paul Giovanni.

"Chad, I have to tell you something," he said.

"What is it, sir?" Chad asked.

"Cut that 'sir' stuff! I don't deserve it."

"But look at what you've tried to achieve for these kids in the Frankenstein Project. And you've been risking your life by—."

"None of that means very much in comparison to what I did *before* I came to know Christ as Savior and Lord."

"Everything has been forgiven," Chad reminded him.

"Does that include the murder of your mother?"

What Giovanni had just said didn't register in Chad's brain.

"I . . . I don't know what you mean." Chad said blankly.

"That I—."

Giovanni looked at him, hating the words that he knew had to come.

"Son, I'm the one who ordered the car bomb that killed your mother," he said finally.

Chad didn't react for the first three seconds, then he lunged for Paul Giovanni, knocking him over on his back. Like a madman, Chad started hitting the man with his fists. Dr. Cosmatos and two other staff members had to pull him off Giovanni.

*"Murderer!"* Chad screamed with red-hot anger. "What reason would you have to kill my mother?"

Giovanni struggled to his feet.

"We were after your father," he said, his voice trembling.

"But you settled for Mom instead?"

"We . . . we thought we had to . . . to send a message. Your father is very smart, very clever. He was getting too close. He had to be stopped."

"But that didn't stop him, did it?" Chad shouted.

*"No!"* Giovanni cried. "But it did send him after the Middle-East terrorists. That took the heat off us. And—."

Chad managed to break away from the staffers trying to restrain him. He was about to attack Giovanni again when the door to the room was flung open and gunshots collapsed part of the suspended ceiling.

# Twenty-five

According to the diagram, there was a portion of the clinic's air-conditioning system that led toward the front of the building in order to cool down the reception room area. Yet, in cramped quarters where each turn down an aluminum tunnel looked like another, Ryan was becoming confused. His emotions kept getting in the way. He needed to be calm so that he could carefully study the diagram and make sure that he didn't become lost in that maze of look-alike tunnels.

In addition to the shock of hearing what he had about his mother, Ryan was beginning to feel bothered by an old problem that he thought he had conquered.

Claustrophobia.

The fear of being closed in without an exit . . . the fear of tight places on all sides. Ryan was certain this must be how it felt to be buried alive.

And yet Ryan knew, then, in that life-or-death situation, that he could do nothing about it except face it as honestly as he could.

He was covered with perspiration.

And he was crying.

*Oh, Lord, Lord, Lord,* he thought as he tried to control the sudden trembling that had spread over his entire body. *I need to deal with what they said about Mom, but I can't just now. But how can I put it aside? Like switching channels on a TV set? Can I just pretend that I didn't hear it at all and concentrate instead on getting out of here and calling for help? If I don't do that, if I fail—.*

He looked at the dark aluminum "walls" around him, imagining for a split second that they had moved in even closer on him.

*I'm trapped here, lost. Please help me. Please show me the way.*

He heard something then, something that seemed like a voice from heaven itself.

An owl, hooting.

That meant he had to be near the outer part of the clinic and not trapped closer to the center of the building or else the owl's call would not have been so clear.

Holding the diagram up to the light that filtered through a nearby grill, Ryan focused on where he thought that sound had come from.

*Ahead! Turn right. Then—!*

He followed what he hoped was his Lord's leading.

Perspiration dripped into his eyes, stinging them, making it difficult for him to see.

And then he stopped.

He saw a grill just a few feet ahead.

And through it came a whiff of fresh air!

His heart started beating faster as he crawled in that direction, hoping that he wasn't mistaken.

When he reached the grill, he peered through it, and saw the reception room below. A window was open, and a moderate breeze was blowing the curtains that hung to either side of it.

As carefully as he could, Ryan pushed against the grill, gradually working loose the screws that fastened it to the wall. Once he could push it aside, he grabbed one end and pulled it into the tunnel so that it wouldn't fall to the ground, and possibly make enough noise that one of Campana's men would come running.

Thankful for a change that his body wasn't bulky like his brother's, he pulled himself through the opening and then dropped to the floor. There was a little noise on impact but not much.

He hurried quickly to the front door and was opening it when he heard a voice shouting after him.

"Kid, how did you—?" whoever it was started to demand.

Ryan had swung the door wide and made it to the front porch when he heard something whiz by his ear—a bullet had been fired at him.

The limousine was still out front.

He tripped and fell, grateful that he did as another shot was fired directly where he had been standing and hit a passenger's side window on the large black Continental.

The bullet bounced right off it, leaving behind only a few scratches.

*Bulletproof!* Ryan thought. *Of course! If I can just get inside and lock all the doors—!*

Something else.

He could use the car phone as originally intended. But now that he had been discovered, he could drive away in the car since he had nothing to lose at that point.

*Chad and the others! How can I leave them behind like that?*

Once inside, he locked the doors, put one key in the ignition, and another in a lock that activated the car phone.

He dialed the special code his father had given him just for emergencies. A voice came on at the receiving end, asking him for identification. He gave the number that identified who his father was and then spouted out everything that had happened.

He took too long.

Two more men had appeared from inside the clinic. Two were carrying machine guns, which they were aiming at the limo.

Ryan turned on the ignition and pushed the gas pedal to the floor. The huge car was built for luxury, not sport-car power, and it stalled.

The two men opened fire.

Ryan got it started again. This time he eased down on the gas pedal, and the limo moved ahead quickly enough.

Something was wrong.

It rode like it had square wheels.

Ryan realized what had happened.

*The tires! The gunmen have hit at least one of the tires, the only part of the limo not bullet-proofed.*

The car swerved.

Ryan couldn't steer it away from a deep, wide ditch that ran along the side of that part of the road.

Ahead a tree.

And he crashed into it, the impact throwing him back against the seat so hard that he could hear part of the frame snap.

He shot a glance through the rearview mirror.

The men were running toward him.

Ryan opened the door and rolled out of the limo onto the ground. Then he scrambled to his feet and ran toward the wooded area just ahead.

He had been in forestland before but never under such circumstances. Every sound somehow seemed a threat to him.

He heard the snapping of twigs and the rustling of leaves in back of him. He had no idea where to go, just that he couldn't allow those men to catch up to him.

He tripped again, got to his feet, and ran straight into a tall, broad man who had a revolver in his hand. The stranger was holding a finger up to his mouth, motioning Ryan to be quiet as he pulled him to one side.

A series of shots were being fired before the two gangsters were ever in sight.

"I'm not alone," the man with Ryan said. "There are two dozen of us in this area."

"But I . . . I just called on the car phone," Ryan said surprised.

"I know. I got the message on my remote. But we've not been far away from the very start. We've been assigned to watch Giovanni for months."

"How come?"

"He's very important to us. And we knew his life could be in danger."

*Of course!* Ryan exclaimed to himself. *Chad and I should have realized that!*

"But why haven't you acted until now?" he asked.

"We weren't sure that anything was wrong actually. Nobody was able to contact us before you did. We didn't go ahead and 'wire' Giovanni with a microphone simply because we couldn't risk its being discovered by the guy's enemies."

"We've got to do something and quick!" Ryan said. "Laurene Giovanni is going to be murdered along with her father."

Ryan stopped himself, realizing that he still felt some concern for the man.

He explained quickly what was happening.

"Move in now, and hurry," the man said into his walkie-talkie after listening to Ryan.

*Hurry,* he repeated the word. *Hurry now . . . and enter the clinic. But what would they find?*

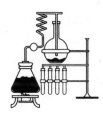 # Twenty-six

All of the men who had betrayed Paul Giovanni to join Tony Campana were captured. Campana himself nearly escaped, but he had been caught just as he was about to enter the forest area around the clinic.

Chad was safe. So was Dr. Cosmatos.

But not Paul Giovanni. And not Laurene Giovanni.

Both had been badly hurt though there was a chance that they might survive.

The two of them were being carried on separate stretchers. Laurene, with blankets over her body to shield her from light, was being taken to a special XP room for emergency care.

Dr. Cosmatos looked deeply worried.

"I don't know what will happen to her," he admitted. "She has a chance to survive, but that doesn't *guarantee* anything. I do know that fluorescent light isn't quite as bad as other kinds—this Campana character obviously didn't realize that—but it's still a serious problem. She was exposed to it for quite a long time. I think she'll survive, but I just can't be sure."

And there was Paul Giovanni himself, on another stretcher. He looked very weak, his face contorted with pain. Tears were streaming down his cheeks as he glanced at Ryan and Chad while being carried past them and into the awaiting ambulance.

Ryan, clearly the more emotional of the two, struggled with feelings of hatred for Giovanni. He almost wished the man had been killed. After all, Giovanni had left them without a mother. He was responsible for their three years of sorrow and loneliness since her tragic death. Ryan wanted to tell the man just what he thought of him. He started to walk toward the stretcher.

"Don't," Chad whispered as he put his hand gently on his brother's shoulder.

"But he might live," Ryan said, not whispering. "He might go on as though nothing has happened. What's his punishment? How can he get by without being punished?"

Chad didn't have the words to provide the answers that his brother so clearly needed.

"I feel so empty, Ryan," he said. "I feel so useless. You need help right now and . . . and I can't give it to you. I—."

The two brothers broke down then, embracing, sobbing to one another as they stood just outside the clinic. Ryan's eyes roamed for a second or two, and he saw Paul Giovanni looking at him just as the ambulance doors were being shut.

"I pray that the little girl will make it," Ryan said as they sat on the front porch of their home the next afternoon. "But I . . . I almost hope Giovanni *doesn't*. I hate to say it, but he deserves whatever happens."

Chad turned, and his gaze met his brother's.

"Don't think that," he said reluctantly, knowing that he still struggled with his own feelings toward Giovanni.

"I know it's wrong, Chad, but I can't help myself. You don't know what he did, you don't—."

"I do."

"How—? I mean—."

"He told me."

"And you're not glad he might die?" Ryan asked.

"Some part of me may have to admit to that, yes," Chad told him. "But there's more, Ryan. We have to forgive him, as Christ forgave us. You realize that, don't you?"

Ryan nodded, but added, "I know it in my *mind*, Chad. But my heart tells me something else. Paul

Giovanni is responsible for Mom's death. How can we just think about that a couple of times and then get over it as though it's just yesterday's news?"

"You don't know what happened last night inside the clinic, Ryan."

"I don't need to know. I—."

"Listen to me, Ryan, listen to every word."

*Laurene was in a room filled with light . . . a room that had been used as a kind of mini gymnasium in the basement of the clinic.*

*All the lights had been turned on. And more were brought in from elsewhere in the building.*

*She sat there tied to a chair, unable to move, unable to escape the harsh, hot, deadly lights.*

*Paul Giovanni went crazy when he saw what was happening to his daughter. He pushed his captors aside and rushed to Laurene's side. That's when he was shot in the back by Tony Campana. But Giovanni managed to get his daughter and untie the ropes restraining her, and she fell into his arms.*

"Ryan?" Chad said.

"Yes . . ." his brother replied.

"Oh, Ryan, it was so awful, so sad. But then something very beautiful happened."

"What?"

"I heard her talking about the light."

*She was smiling, in spite of her overwhelming weakness and intense pain.*

"Daddy," she said, her voice surprisingly strong. "The light. . . ."

"Yes, yes, my beloved," her father said, his own voice weak with pain.

"There's a stranger standing in the middle of it," she continued. "He has such a kind face, Daddy. Don't you see Him?"

"No, dearest Laurene, I don't—."

Tears were streaming down Chad's cheeks.

"I think he was about to tell her that there was no stranger, that he saw no one when suddenly—."

Paul Giovanni's eyes lit up, as though filled with a light source of their own.

"Daddy, you see Him now, don't you?" Laurene was saying as they were holding one another, both of them on the hardwood floor of the gymnasium.

She kissed her father on the cheek.

"You don't have to feel bad anymore, Daddy," she told him. "He just said something about—."

"—forgiveness," he finished the sentence for her.

"You heard Him, too?" she replied, hugging Giovanni around the neck.

Laurene seemed to gasp then, ever so quietly and passed out. Her body became limp, looking somehow like a delicate little doll waiting for someone to pick her up and love her again.

Paul Giovanni let out one cry as he turned and looked at Tony Campana who was standing not *far away. It was obvious at first that Giovanni wanted to reach out and strangle his former friend-turned-traitor. Then something happened—within the mobster. And the change was visible on the outside. In an instant, his whole manner went from hatred to something else, something as different as could be imagined.*

Chad could hardly continue for the emotions that were assaulting him.

"Ryan . . . he . . . he . . . said something then that I won't forget, no matter how long I live. He said—."

"*—All my days, as far back as I can remember, I took an eye for an eye, a tooth for a tooth, a life for a life, Tony.*" *Giovanni's voice was barely above a whisper, strained by the pain he was experiencing.* "*But, now—.*"

*He motioned for Campana to come closer. Hesitantly, a revolver in his hand, the other man approached the large, fallen body.*

"*No!*" *Campana said after hearing what Giovanni wanted to tell him.* "*You can't mean that. You—.*"

*He aimed the revolver at Giovanni and pulled the trigger, but the shot missed and hit the floor instead.*

"*I hate you,*" *Campana said.* "*This is your way of getting back at me, of trying to make me feel—.*"

"Paul Giovanni lost consciousness then," Chad

was saying. "Campana dropped the gun and wandered off. When they found him, he had been trying to escape through the woods. As they put handcuffs on him, he was muttering something over and over."

*"I can't accept his forgiveness. There's no such thing for me. I can't let him get away with—."*

*He looked at the men on either side of him.*

*"—I can't let him get away with forgiving me! After what I did? After what I've always done—?"*

Both Chad and Ryan were silent for a few moments.

Finally Ryan spoke.

"I can hate Paul Giovanni," he said. "That's easy. We live alone most of the time because of him. I still see images of Mom at the breakfast table, in the backyard where she used to do her gardening, at church in the spot beside us that's empty now . . . *so empty!*"

He buried his head in his hands, sobbing fitfully.

"And . . . and out front where . . . where the car was. The stains are gone, Chad, you and I know that. But we see them everyday in our minds when we leave for school . . . we—."

It was hard to forgive . . . so very hard.

## DON'T MISS THESE OTHER BARTLETT BROTHER ADVENTURES:

### Sudden Fear

When Ryan Bartlett accidently intercepts a computer message, he and his brother are stalked by terrorists, who plan to destroy a nuclear power plant. (ISBN 0–8499–3301–3)

### Terror Cruise

The Bartlett family embarks on a Caribbean cruise that is supposed to be a time of rest and relaxation, but instead becomes a journey into terror. (ISBN 0–8499–3302–1)

### Forbidden River

The brothers find themselves in the midst of the war on drugs, with corruption and danger stretching from South America's Forbidden River to the U.S. Congress. (ISBN 0–8499–3304–8)

# ABOUT THE AUTHOR

Award-winning author Roger Elwood is well known for his suspense-filled stories for both youth and adult readers. His twenty-six years of editing and writing experience include stories in *Today's Youth* and *Teen Life* magazines and a number of best-selling novels for Scholastic Book Clubs and Weekly Reader Book Clubs. He has also had titles featured by Junior Literary Guild and Science Fiction Book Club. Among his most outstanding adult books is *Angelwalk*, a winner of the Angel Award from Religion in Media.